Disney · PIXAR
TURNING RED

D0004027

♥MEI'S WILD RIDE☁

adapted by Natasha Bouchard

illustrated by the Disney Storybook Art Team

Random House 🏠 New York

Meilin Lee and her mother
are very close.
Mei and Ming
do everything together.

Mei also likes spending time
with her best friends,
Abby, Priya, and Miriam.

Miriam, Priya, and Abby

admire the store clerk, Devon.

But Mei is not impressed.

Mei reminds her friends
that 4*Town is the best.
4*Town is their favorite
music group.

Mei rushes home.

She likes helping her mom

at their family temple.

Mei honors her ancestors.
One is Sun Yee, the guardian
of the red pandas.

Later, Mei thinks about Devon.

She doodles pictures

of them together in her notebook.

Ming sees Mei's drawings.

She is shocked!

Furious, Ming takes Mei
to Devon's store.
Ming confronts Devon
and shows him Mei's notebook.
Ming warns Devon to stay away
from her daughter.

Mei feels sad, mad,
and embarrassed.

The next morning,
Mei is not a teenage girl.
She has transformed into
a giant red panda!

Mei tries to calm down.

She takes a deep breath.

Poof! She is a girl again.

But now she has red hair.

Ming knows something is wrong.

She follows Mei to school.

This embarrasses Mei.

She poofs back into

a big red panda!

Ming sees it happen.

Ming tells Mei their family secret.
Every woman in their family
can transform into a red panda.

She and Mei will perform a ritual
to seal the red panda spirit
into a talisman on the night
of a red moon.

Mei doesn't know what to do.

She tells her best friends

everything.

They comfort her.

Suddenly, Mei poofs

back into a girl.

Mei's friends help her stay calm.

4*Town is having a concert!

But Ming forbids Mei from going.

The friends make a secret plan

to earn money for concert tickets.

They take photos with classmates.

They sell red panda souvenirs.

Everyone loves the red panda!

Mei's family arrives
to plan the ritual.
Mei's grandma wants to make sure
the ritual is successful.
Mei must behave until then.

But Ming finds out
about the secret concert plans.
She blames Priya, Miriam,
and Abby for Mei's behavior.
Mei feels ashamed.

A few days later,

it is time for the ritual.

Mei's family gathers around her.

Mei floats in the air.

A bright light flashes!

In the Astral Realm,

Mei steps through a magical mirror.

She sees her red panda spirit.

She thinks about all her memories

with the red panda.

Mei does not want to lose
the red panda spirit.
She wants to keep both
her good and messy sides.
She returns to her world.

Mei escapes from her family.

She finds her friends

at the concert.

They are proud of Mei

for being true to herself.

Ming is angry because

Mei has disobeyed her.

Ming turns into a huge red panda!

She finds Mei at the concert

and destroys the stage!

Mei flies at Ming, stopping
her mother in her tracks.
The red moon is fading fast.
Mei's family arrives
to perform the ritual again.

In the Astral Realm,

Ming lets go of her panda spirit.

But Mei keeps her red panda.

Ming finally accepts

that Mei is growing up.

Her daughter needs to be herself.

Mei knows that her family and friends
will always be there for her.
She finally feels confident
to be herself—with both
her good and messy sides!

© Disney/Pixar

4*Town 4*Eva

PANDA POWER!

I GOT THIS!

PANDA MODE ACTIVATED!

Besties 4ever

Freakin' Adorable

TO CUTE TO HANDLE